John Bishop

The Hunterian Oration

Anatiposi

John Bishop

The Hunterian Oration

Reprint of the original.

1st Edition 2023 | ISBN: 978-3-38230-498-0

Anatiposi Verlag is an imprint of Outlook Verlagsgesellschaft mbH.

Verlag (Publisher): Outlook Verlag GmbH, Zeilweg 44, 60439 Frankfurt, Deutschland
Vertretungsberechtigt (Authorized to represent): E. Roepke, Zeilweg 44, 60439 Frankfurt, Deutschland
Druck (Print): Books on Demand GmbH, In de Tarpen 42, 22848 Norderstedt, Deutschland

THE

HUNTERIAN ORATION

DELIVERED AT

THE ROYAL COLLEGE OF SURGEONS OF ENGLAND,

On FEBRUARY 14TH, 1859,

BY

JOHN BISHOP, F.R.S., F.R.C.S.,

MEMBER OF THE COUNCIL OF THE ROYAL COLLEGE OF SURGEONS OF
ENGLAND, CONSULTING SURGEON TO THE NORTHERN DISPENSARY,
LATE SENIOR SURGEON TO THE ISLINGTON DISPENSARY,
CORRESPONDING MEMBER OF THE MEDICAL
SOCIETIES OF BERLIN AND MADRID, ETC.

LONDON:
JOHN CHURCHILL, NEW BURLINGTON STREET.

1859.

TO

JOSEPH HENRY GREEN, ESQ., F.R.S.

PRESIDENT OF THE ROYAL COLLEGE OF SURGEONS
OF ENGLAND,

𝔗𝔥𝔦𝔰 𝔒𝔯𝔞𝔱𝔦𝔬𝔫 𝔦𝔰 𝔇𝔢𝔡𝔦𝔠𝔞𝔱𝔢𝔡

AS A TESTIMONY OF HIS SINCERE ESTEEM AND
RESPECT,

BY THE AUTHOR.

38, BERNARD STREET,
    RUSSELL SQUARE. 1859.

HUNTERIAN ORATION.

Mr. President,

After the many able and eloquent Addresses which have been delivered from this place on similar occasions, and after the publication of the several Memoirs of John Hunter, in which every circumstance, however minute, relating to him has been given to the world, I feel very sensibly the difficulty there would be in throwing any additional light on his biography. His writings, although so numerous, so varied, and so extensive, have from the period of his death to the present day been subjected to the closest scrutiny and criticism. Instead, therefore, of narrating at length what has been so often repeated, and which must be so familiar to all those who have taken any interest in the biography and writings of Hunter, it appears to me more advantageous that I

In publishing this Oration the Author has taken the liberty to introduce a few sentences which, with a view to economise time, were omitted in the delivery.

should report to you the state and the progress that has been made in those sciences from which we derive our knowledge of the functions of animal life, and also the advance that has more recently been effected in some of the researches of which Hunter laid the foundation, and in which he pointed out the processes by which farther investigation should be conducted.

It is well known that Hunter at the age of 20, commmenced his studies in Anatomy and Physiology under his brother, Dr. William Hunter, and that he completed his surgical studies under Cheselden and Pott. It would have been difficult to have selected, at that period, three individuals in London who were better qualified to lay the foundation of those researches in every department of that Science of which Hunter afterwards became so distinguished a cultivator.

It would be doing great injustice to John Hunter were we to institute a comparison between his opinions on various subjects, (many of which were merely hypothetical, and expressed fifty years ago) and those entertained at the present day, more especially as during this latter period all branches of the natural and physical sciences have made such rapid and extraordinary progress. If, however, we should desire to estimate the claims of Hunter as compared with those of his predecessors or contemporaries, we might in vain seek to find his equal.

In order to form a correct estimate of Hunter's

real claims to the great reputation which is to this day accorded to him, we need only turn our eyes to the splendid collection of physiological preparations in the Museum of this College, and read and study the scope and bearing of his numerous writings on the animal economy, on physiology, pathology, and surgery, to become convinced that he was endowed with so great an amount of untiring zeal and industry, so comprehensive and vigorous an intellect, and so vast a range of genius and talent, as have never been equalled since the time of Aristotle.

Among the predecessors of Hunter, no one has exceeded in talent the transcendent and diversified genius of Aristotle, the lustre of whose name has not been dimmed by the lapse of nearly 20 centuries.

We are told by Hunter's biographer and relative, Sir Everard Home, that the principal object he had in view in the formation of his splendid and unrivalled physiological collection was "to institute an inquiry into the various organizations by which the functions of life are performed, that he might acquire some knowledge of the general principles of the animal economy." With this view he pursued his physiological dissections throughout all the classes of the animal kingdom. He very properly conceived that by tracing out the structure and functions of the organs which maintain life in the simplest forms of animals, he would arrive by induction at a knowledge of the functions of the organs which exist in the more complex and elaborate mechanism of Man, and he aspired, by following this process, to arrive at a knowledge of the nature of the vital principle itself.

In all his researches Hunter did not rest contented with simply describing the phenomena which present themselves to the observer in the several processes of the animal economy, whether relating to Physiology or Pathology, but he aimed at the discovery of the causes which produce them, and he endeavoured to trace out the relations existing between the normal and the abnormal states of the body in every department of surgical inquiry. That he accomplished so much in this wide field of research cannot but excite our admiration : that he was not always successful is to be ascribed rather to the difficult nature of his inquiries than to any want on his part of industry, or of mental acumen.

Hunter, by an extensive series of experiments, investigated the nature of every object which came within the scope of his inquiries, and his conclusions were deduced in accordance with his investigations, rather than from the state in which Physiology and Pathology existed at that period.

In collecting his materials from a multitude of observations and experiments, and in deducing his conclusions from them, rather than from the vague theories and hypotheses for explaining the functions of animal life which were at that time current, and thus extending to Physiology and Pathology the system of induction founded by Bacon, Hunter may be considered as having achieved for these sciences what the former had effected for the natural sciences in general.

In the splendid Address delivered at Grantham, at the inauguration of the statue of Newton, Lord Brougham states that "Cuvier had been preceded by inquirers who took sound views of fossil osteology, among whom the truly original genius of Hunter fills the foremost place." And in another Address delivered in New York, Dr. Francis says—"The world has produced but one Aristotle, one Bacon, one Newton, one Franklin, one Washington, and one John Hunter."

These examples are sufficient evidence of the high estimation in which the labours of Hunter are held beyond the pale of the profession, and on the other side of the Atlantic.

Hunter never resorted to hypothesis when the nature of the subject admitted of demonstrative proof, either of an anatomical or physiological nature ; and he thus laid the basis for a more accurate method of inquiry, and raised Surgery from an empirical art to an exalted science, embracing the study of the relations and transitions subsisting between the normal and abnormal functions of the body.

The important discoveries made by Hunter, and the principles he laid down, are quite sufficient to immortalize his name without ascribing to him infallibility, a gift to which no mortal can lay claim. The soundness of his views on several questions of Surgery and Pathology may be estimated by the fact that in the settlement of disputed points, he is often at the present day referred to as the highest authority; but as all branches of science are progressive, we must not rest contented to receive the views either of Hunter, or of any other authority as the final condition of these sciences.

The train of thought by which Hunter was led to the formation of the great series of anatomical and physiological preparations collected in our Museum being now understood, we may easily conceive that considerations of a similar kind have operated in all other anatomical collections; and hence it may be affirmed that the contents of a museum may furnish us with an indication of the design of the curator; and this proposition we find exemplified, not only in the Hunterian collection, but also in the collections of every museum in Europe, such as those of Amsterdam, Berlin, Paris, &c.

Although many of the foreign museums contain a more perfect collection of particular series of preparations, the Hunterian museum is far more rich in choice specimens; and, taken as a whole, may be regarded as being of equal, if not of superior importance to any in Europe.

For a long period it has been a matter of serious consideration with the Council to effect the completion of the Catalogue of the Museum. This great undertaking has been in hand for upwards of fifty years. The destruction of Mr. Hunter's papers by Sir Everard Home has rendered this a work of more than ordinary toil and difficulty, requiring talents of more than ordinary range. It has now happily been brought to a successful termination by the united labours of Clift, Owen, Paget, Morris, and Queckett, names which afford sufficient guarantees for the fidelity and intrinsic value of these volumes. This will no doubt be appreciated by the students and visitors of the museum. Before the completion of the catalogue the museum was of comparatively little value to the student.

The Zoological classification of the collection occupied much of Hunter's attention, but he did not succeed in forming a system more general in its application than that proposed by Aristotle and adopted by Linnæus, founded on the colour of the blood, or on its equivalent more recently introduced by Lamarck, namely, the vertebrate and invertebrate series. It is according to the latter system that the Hunterian museum is now arranged. The theory of an archetype or plan on which the four great divisions of the animal kingdom are based, the laws of progressive development, and the controversy of the transmutation or non-transmutation of species, are subjects which are engrossing the attention of speculative zoologists of the present day.

The College has faithfully discharged the trust reposed in it by the Government for the management and careful preservation of the Hunterian collection, which is pronounced by competent judges, Professors Owen and Queckett, to be at the present time in a better state of preservation than it was fifty years ago. The College has already increased the number of anatomical preparations to more than three times those originally collected by Hunter, and and they now amount to nearly forty-five thousand. Of these, more than fourteen thousand are microscopic, and were prepared, or collected by Professor Queckett : among these are found the valuable and matchless results of the dissections of the nervous system by Lenhossék.

Since we were last assembled on this occasion, the profession has had to deplore the loss of two of its most distinguished members, Robert Keate, and Benjamin Travers.

Both these able and justly esteemed Surgeons had occupied the offices of President of the College, and Members of the Council and of the Court of Examiners, all of which they filled with great ability and inflexible integrity. The cultivated talent, the gentlemanly deportment, and the unblemished reputation of these two members of our profession would have claimed a more lengthened exposition of their intrinsic merit, had not their memoirs, already published, handed down to posterity a record of their characters, talents, writings, and claims to our veneration and regard,

The question whether Life is the result of organization, or organization the result of Life, a question which has occupied the attention of philosophers from the time of Aristotle to the present day, is a problem still unsolved. No very clear conception seems to have been formed respecting what would be a correct and satisfactory definition of Life. The investigation of the nature of the Vital Force has been attempted by Buffon, Cuvier, Bichât, Blainville, Schelling, Müller, Whewell, and Hunter, most of whom concur in the doctrine that the phenomena of Life resembles a vortex in which each particle, while whirling, is constantly changing its form.

The idea that Life or Vital Force is a subtile, sentient agent which presides over the several vegetative functions of the body, is an opinion that has prevailed for many centuries, and has arisen from the metaphysical conceptions of the middle ages, but is an idea which is now giving way to the advances recently made in physical science. Mr. Grove has shewn that there is a " correlation existing between Light, Heat, Electricity, and Magnetism,". and he proves also "their convertibility into each other," and it is now believed, and with good reason, that the nervous system is operated on by one or more forms of the Forces, without the agency of which neither plants can germinate nor animals live. That Heat is one of the Forces that exerts this essential agency is now generally admitted. Hunter, after comparing Life to Magnetism, remarks that " Heat is one of the first principles of Action in Nature," thus foreshadowing what science has since tended to establish.

The science of Optics has shared in the advance which has been made in every branch of Physics,

One of its applications is the vast improvement in the construction of the microscope, the increased powers of which have greatly assisted our investigation of Structural Anatomy and Pathology, and it may be considered to have produced as great a revolution in our knowledge of Histology, as the telescope as done in that of Astronomy. By the aid of this instrument, the cells from which all animal tissues are derived were discovered, and the cell theory founded. Bodies presenting a surface not greater than the 100,000th part of an inch admit of being examined; and now that many of the organic changes may be observed during their occurrence in living animals, it is obvious that our physiological and pathological knowledge has been greatly extended by the use of that instrument. But as there is a limit to the space-penetrating power of the largest telescope, so is there likewise a limit to the highest powers of the microscope. It fails to make us acquainted with the ultimate molecules of matter which are assumed by mathematicians to be inconceivably minute.

The pathology of Inflammation, which occupied so much of Hunter's attention has since been farther investigated by Travers, Wharton Jones, Lister, and Virchow, and from their researches we have obtained more correct views than had previously been entertained of the pathology of inflammatory affections. According to Virchow and Ilis, many of the supposed exudations of inflammatory actions are really nothing more than the products of metamorphosed local tissues.*

It has been found by Ollier that the Periosteum is capable of generating bone when engrafted on any of the tissues of the living organism ; and Harley's researches prove that the supra-renal capsules are not essential to life, and that they have no influence on the colour of the skin as had been supposed by Dr. Addison.

It is now 114 years since the barbers and surgeons of England agreed, from the incompatibility of their several pursuits, to divide partnership, and each to take their respective station. Surgery had already more or less assumed a higher and more scientific character by the necessity of dealing with operations on the living organism, and the result has been, that while one occupation remains a trade of no very elevated character, the other has gained a position due to the exalted rank of the science it professes to cultivate, and to the benefit it confers on the public.

Haller expressed surprise that up to his time Surgeons had remained undistinguished characters ; but this reproach has long since been removed, as the names of Cheselden, Pott, Hunter, and Abernethy among those of the past epoch will suffice to prove. Dundas, Home, Cooper, and Brodie have been created baronets, and during the past year, one of our members, Sir Benjamin Brodie, has been elected to the

* Microscopic Journal, October 1857. page 55.

highest honor that science can bestow, the Presidency of the Royal Society, and another member, Professor Owen, has been chosen the President of the British Association,

The bill that has recently passed the legislature has conferred on the Medical Profession the right of self-government, untrammelled by state interference; constituting that liberty of action which is the only real foundation for the progress and development of art and science. It has not only preserved the existing rights and privileges of this college, but it has conferred on its members rights and immunities which they did not before possess. The government, also, sensible at length of the importance of engaging the services of well educated Surgeons in the Army, has increased both their rank and emoluments to a scale more commensurate with the claims of the surgical profession : and most assuredly the Naval Surgeons are equally deserving of the same consideration.

As the progress of civilization and the education of the profession advance, and the true interests of the human race are better understood, we may indulge in the hope that the time is not far distant when the social station of those whose province it is to preserve life, will be raised to a state of equality with that of those whose business it is to destroy it: that honors may be conferred on the professors of medical science as freely as on those of the military, legal and clerical professions; honors, which are justly due to the noble and sublime sciences they cultivate, and the extensive benefits they confer on mankind.

The sciences from which we may expect to derive a more exact knowledge of the general functions of organic life, after having acquired a perfect knowledge of Anatomy, are chiefly Statics, Dynamics, Chemistry, and the various forms of Electro-Magnetism. Among those who have contributed to render Physiology an exact science, we find the names of some of the greatest and most illustrious Mathematicians who have ever lived to adorn and enlighten the human race. We have the contributions of Newton, Borelli, Euler, Daniel Bernouilli, Poisson, Weber, Thomas Young, Gompertz, Challis, Donders, Valentin, Volkmann, and Draper, By the united labours of these distinguished philosophers we have already obtained the solution of a great number of problems in the physics of Physiology.

While Rœmer was engaged in observing the eclipses of Jupiter's satellites by which the velocity of Light was measured, and Newton was employed in the investigation of the laws of Gravitation; while at the same time mathematicians were endeavouring to solve the problem of the co-existence of small vibrations, it was little imagined that Physiology would have to avail itself of these discoveries for the determination of the nature of several phenomena in animal Physiology. Two or three examples will suffice. As soon as Sir Isaac Newton had accomplished the decomposition of white light into different coloured rays and had succeeded in measuring the length of their several undulations, he immediately suggested the probability that the sensation and perception of different colours depend on the number of undulations entering the eye in a unit of time : this hypothesis has since been verified, and the numbers computed by Young and Frauenhofer.

These researches lead to all we know on the production of the sense of colour in Vision. Newton also foreshadowed the idea of the relation subsisting between the senses of Vision and Hearing; and, more recently, the number of undulations corresponding to the sensations of certain sounds and colours has been determined by Young and by Mosotti.

The manner in which the Ear is constructed, so as to enable a person to hear a great number of sounds at the same time, is a question, which has long embarrassed Physiologists. This subject has been investigated by Euler and Duhamel. The former founded his calculations on the hypothesis that sounds reach the ear from different distances with the same velocity at different times. Duhamel, on the contrary, supposed that all sounds affect the ear at the same time, and that all the undulations superpose each other without interference, on the principle of the superposition or co-existence of small motions.

Weber has shown that different parts of the surface of the body are endowed with different degrees of sensibility, and that the power of the sense of Touch to appreciate minute differences between two points,

varies in proportion to the number of nervous fila-
ments distributed to the skin.   Poisson, Weber, and
Professor Thury have estimated the vis viva, or force
expended during progression : according to the latter
the force produced for each metre $= 7\frac{9}{10}$ kilogrammes ;
and Weber has demonstrated that in locomotion the
legs are oscillated by gravity like the pendulum of a
clock, without the aid of muscular force.

Daniel Bernouilli* has demonstrated that the smal-
ler the angle between the ribs and spine, the greater
is the tension of the intercostal muscles in raising the
ribs.   The force of the heart in the circulation of the
blood has been investigated theoretically by Challis,
and Young, and experimentally by Poiseulle, Valentin,
and by Volkmann.   Gompertz† has investigated the
laws of the decrement of the vital power, and has
given a formula for estimating the length of life,
which agrees in a remarkable manner with the laws
of mortality.   Notwithstanding the success which
has resulted from the mathematical labours of these
illustrious investigators, too little attention has been
given to them by the medical profession, and there
are to be found at the present day some who appear
neither to have the taste to appreciate, nor the talent
to comprehend the relations subsisting between the
physiological and the mathematical sciences.

The solution of the whole of the problems in the

* Dissertatio inauguralis Physico-Medicam, De Respiratione.—Daniel
Bernouilli, Basil, 1721.

† Phil. Trans. 1825.

physics of animal physiology will terminate human labour in that direction. The student will then only have to comprehend and apply them. This end should always be kept in view, and, however distant the prospect, its attainment is apparently neither improbable nor impossible. Those who attempt to prosecute these researches must be qualified by a knowledge of the laws which regulate and govern inorganic matter in their most profound aspect. It should not be forgotten that what has been already accomplished has been effceted by those whose talents and education were of the highest order—by mathematicians who had successfully cultivated the physical sciences before attempting researches in Physiology. Our belief in the possibility of future investigations placing Physiology on a level with the exact sciences is strengthened by what has been already effected.

It is the boast of Physioiogy that our researches are conducted by the pure method of *induction*, as inculcated by Bacon ; but the truth of our inferences by induction often requires to be proved by *deduction* with the aid of algebra or geometry ; for, without this, our conclusions on many subjects command no respect beyond that which attaches to the mere assumptions of hypotheses, whether these may be true or false.

The notions of vital and hyper-physical actions have too long proved stumbling blocks to scientific investigations in all that relates to animal Physiology. This becomes apparent in every discovery made either in the mechanical, the chemical, or the electrical functions of animal life. If there be not an alliance of the physiological with the physical sciences, how does it happen that the mathematician examines the eye and ear, and the physiologist the nature of light and sound, in order to explain the senses of sight and of hearing?

If the mathematician experiences great difficulty in dealing with the problems presented in the dynamics of animal physiology, the chemist finds himself no less embarrassed with the solution of those chemical changes which are incessantly taking place in the functions of vegetable and animal life.

It is admitted that chemical science cannot reach the explanation of the mechanical and chemical processes in living organs until the laws of molecular forces have been determined. On this point Professor Hopkins observes that " Molecular actions present to the mathematician problems of a higher order than any that have been solved in gravitation," and that " the problems of the vital actions present infinitely greater difficulties still." Such then are the conditions for the process and the prospects of a final solution of this problem.

The ideas which have prevailed in all historical time of the hyper-chemical nature of organic changes have materially operated in retarding the successful cultivation of physiological and pathological chemistry ; and it is only within the last ten years that the chemists of Germany, France, and England began seriously to apply chemical science to these branches of knowledge.

Nearly all the organic compounds have been reduced to their elementary principles by chemical analysis; but chemical science has lain under the reproach of not being able to unite them again by synthesis. Hitherto no chemist has succeeded in forming albumen; those, however, who believe that all organic changes are hyper-chemical, have been startled by the announcement that Wöller had succeeded in transforming cyanate of ammonia into urea. This is the first example of the transformation of an inorganic into an organic compound.

The mathematical formula for the atomic elements of the several Protein bodies is the same; but the physical differences between Albumen, Casein, and Fibrin, are well known. The metamorphoses of Protein bodies into Chondrin, Gelatin, Sintonin, and Globulin, the molecular changes and the transformations from which these substances result, are problems which Chemical Science has not yet reached, If the physical change in the coagulation of Albumen by heat has not yet been determined, we need not be surprised that the cause of the coagulation of the blood baffled Hunter, embued as Physiology in his time was with the doctrine of the " Life of the Blood," which had been the prevailing idea of physiologists from the period of the earliest history, from the time of the great Jewish lawgiver and the Pharaohs, to that of Harvey, Hunter, and their immediate successors.

It has long been known that the caustic Alkalies and their Carbonates have power to prevent the coagulation of blood by their action on the fibrine; and recently Dr. Richardson has discovered that the coagulation is accompanied by the escape of Ammonia, thus shewing the nature of the change to be a chemical, instead of a vital process

The chemical effects of the salivary, gastric, pancreatic, and biliary secretions have been investigated by Valentin, Eberle, Harvey, and Bernard; and the secretions which act on the Protein, and those which act on the Carbo-hydrated substances have been clearly resolved.

Valentin has discovered that the pancreatic, like the salivary fluid, transforms starch into sugar. Eberle found that the pancreatic fluid converts fatty substances into emulsions, and Harley supposes that it acts on the Albumen. The gastric juice dissolves the Protein substances, and transforms them into Pepsine, and it also changes the fats into fatty acids; and since Bernard discovered the formation of sugar in the liver, Dr. Marcet has found that the bile assists in changing fatty substances into emulsions, by which they are capable of entering into the composition of the chyle. Dr. Theophilus Thompson and others find that the fats and oils are essentially necessary for the transformation of the chyle corpuscles into the blood corpuscles.

Dr. Draper has shewn that the influence of the force of endosmose is sufficient to account for all the processes of absorption; and he finds that this force depends on the electro-chemical relation subsisting between the fluids and solids in contact with each other. This force of endosmose is sufficient to overcome the resistance of from ten to twenty-five atmospheres, and will cause fluids to permeate the porous tissues of organs whose apertures are too minute to be detected even with the highest powers of the microscope.

Vierordt has made a series of experiments with a view to determine the variation in the amount of carbonic acid depending on the number and duration of the respiratory movements; and his conclusions are that it would require 300 respirations in a minute for the entire removal of the carbon from the blood.

Bidder, Schmidt, and Dr. Edward Smith have investigated the influence of different kinds of food on the expiration of carbonic acid. Vierordt found that the carbonic acid was diminished during the period of fasting.

The results of Dr. Smith's experiments, conducted on a more extended scale, corroborate those of Vierordt and others, namely, that the carbonic acid respired decreases in amount as the temperature increases; but he finds that it varies at different seasons of the year under the same degree of heat.

The solution of the problem of the quantity and quality of food, conducted on the principle that the requirements of nutrition are regulated by the amount of the loss of the system, has paved the way to a variety of very important and interesting experiments, among which those by Boussingault, Liebig, Valentin, and Vierordt are worthy of the attentive consideration of the Physiologist.

The chemical components of the mineral and vegetable poisons have been long since analysed, and their physiological effects have been examined by Sir Benjamin Brodie, Orfila, Kölliker, Christison, Taylor and Harley, Recent events have tended to direct public attention to this subject, which is one of great interest in Medical Jurisprudence, as well as in the progress of Physiology.

Since it is found that muscles retain their power of contracting after the nerves which supply them have been destroyed by poison, we are reminded of the " Vis Insita" of Haller.

Although so much attention has been paid to the mineral and vegetable poisons, comparatively little has been done to ascertain the nature of those gaseous poisons, arising from putrefaction, which float in the atmosphere, and which annually destroy thousands of lives. The reports of the Registrar-General on the destruction of life from zymotic causes, and from over-crowded dwellings, have at length awakened public attention to the necessity of appointing persons qualified to deal with the principles and details of sanatory science. The law affecting the health of populations where the numbers in a given space differ, has been ascertained to vary at the $\frac{1}{6}$th root of the density; and the Council of the College, with a view to improve the sanatory condition of our hospitals, has directed that each patient should have the space allotted to him increased from 800 to 1,000 cubic feet.

The discovery by Galvani of the power of producing muscular contractions in a dead animal by means of Electricity led Physiologists to believe they had discovered a Vital Power, and induced Physicians to explain all kinds of nervous diseases, and to announce that henceforward no person could be buried alive if he were galvanized. The idea which arose in the minds of philosophers that the nervous system was endowed with electro-motive power was entertained by Dr. Wilson Philip, Sir John Herschel, Faraday, and others, long before its truth was established. Hunter examined the anatomical structure of the electric apparatus of the Gymnotus, and describes it as consisting of forty-eight prismatic canals on each side, or ninety-six in all, each of these ninety-six piles containing 4,000 diaphragms, thereby forming a prodigiously powerful voltaic pile.

After Matteucci had discovered an electric current proper to the *muscles*, it was reserved for Du Bois Reymond to find a similar current in the *nerves*. This was accomplished by constructing an electrometer of great sensitiveness by a coil of wires of 5,580 yards, or upwards of three miles in length. The direction of the current was from the origin towards the termination of the nerve in the muscle. He assumes that it is produced by electro-motive molecules in the nerves. These molecules are supposed to turn their positive poles in the direction of the current, and their negative poles in the opposite direction. He calls this the electrotonic state of the nerve.

When at length an electric current was found to traverse the nerves, it was imagined that the velocity of its transmission must be as great as in the wires of an electric telegraph; but the experiments of Helmholtz on the frog have shewn that this velocity is very small, not exceeding from 100 to 170 feet in a second, and, according to Séquard, it is not in man more than 3,000 feet in a second. This is owing to the nerves being very imperfect conductors of electricity. The velocity is found to increase with the increase of temperature.

It is supposed by Ritter and Ermann that on closing the galvanic circuit which causes the contraction of the muscle, the nerve passes into another state; andthat, on breaking the circuit, the contraction is produced by the return of the nerve to its original state. By altering the direction of the current rapidly, the nerve is brought into a state of tetanus. After a lengthened series of researches, Reymond concludes that the muscles and nerves as well as the brain and spinal cord are endowed during life with an electro-motive power.

Since, then, every chemical change in the body, every muscular contraction, and every exertion of nervous action is accompanied by a development of electric force, we are driven to the inference that animal life is associated with electro-motive actions, presenting for investigation a numerous series of problems in electro-statics and electro-dynamics, a few only of which have been solved, leaving many for future research.

Since the discovery of the functions of the anterior and posterior roots of the spinal nerves by Sir Charles Bell, and that of the reflex function by Dr. Marshall Hall, the anatomy and physiology of the cerebro-spinal axis has occupied the attention of a host of investigators. Among those who have lately contributed to the advancement of this branch of science may be mentioned the names of Kölliker, Müller, Valentin, Stilling, Arnold, Rolando, Volkmann, Solly, Lockhart Clarke, Nunnely, Lenhossék, and Brown Séquard.

The discovery of the means of rendering the materials of the nervous system transparent is due to Lockhart Clarke;* and it has enabled the Histologist to examine by the microscope, with great advantage, the minute structure of all the cerebro-spinal elements. The nerve cells of the grey and of the white substances, as well as those of the tubular structure of the brain can now, by this means, be easily seen. The course of the sensitive and motor nerves has, in some cases, been traced to their origin; and their modes of connection and decussation in the spinal column have been partly made out. The prolongations of the nerve cells, termed by Stannius their *Poles*, have

*Phil. Trans. 1857.

been traced into the fibres of the nerves ; and thus
the connection between the nerve cells and nerve
cylinders has been established. It must, however, be
borne in mind, that the poles of Stannius, and the
poles of the nerve molecules are quite different in
their anatomical character. The number of nerve
cells is stated by Lockhart Clarke to be in direct
proportion to the size of the nerve roots; and he finds
that all the nerve fibres of the grey substance are of
a tubular structure, and not simply fibres, as hitherto
supposed.

No one of the present period appears to have
contributed more largely to the elucidation of the
functions of the nervous centres than Brown Séquard;
and his experimental inquiries on the functions of
the spinal cord and Medulla Oblongata are of great
practical value, since they will enable us to form a
more correct diagnosis of the seat of the various
lesions affecting these nervous centres than hereto-
fore. He has shewn that the impressions made on
one side of the body are transmitted to the sensorium
on the opposite side of the spinal cord, and that,
consequently, the sensitive fibres running from the
trunk and the limbs, do not decussate in the Medulla
Oblongata, Pons Varolii, Corpora-quadragemina, or
Crura-Cerebri, as had been formerly supposed. He
has also shewn that the posterior columns do not
transmit sensitive impressions[*] to the sensorium as

* A conclusion to which Lockhart Clarke had previously arrived from his
anatomical researches. Phil. Trans. 1853.

had been stated by Sir C. Bell, but that this is a function of a segment of the central grey matter of the cord ; also that every segment of the recipient and conductive elements of the spinal cord is capable of the reception and transmission of sensitive impressions from every part of the body with which it is connected. He has shewn that death does not immediately follow the extirpation of *"the vital point"* of Floureus; that epilepsy depends on the reflex excitability of the cerebro-spinal axis; and he is of opinion that the reflex function acts perpendicularly to the axis of the cord, and resides principally in the posterior columns.

The histological elements of the Medulla Oblongata have also been recently examined by Lockhart Clarke. It appears to be the centre of antomatic action, and on it the functions of respiration and deglutition depend. The Brain may be removed above, and the spinal cord below this nervous centre as far as the origin of the Phrenic nerve without producing death. It exhibits the property of reflex action; and when sensation and voluntary motion have been arrested by breathing Chloroform, the action of the Medulla oblongata survives its effects.

The functions of the Cerebellum have been made the subject of experiment by Rolando, Flourens, Magendie, and others; but they are as yet the subject of controversy. The same uncertainty prevails respecting the functions of the Pons Varolii.

In passing to the Physiology of the cerebral hemispheres we arrive at those organs which are the seat of all the intellectual functions, and thus we proceed from Physiology to Psychology : this branch of science has been recently investigated by Sir Benjamin Brodie, Robert Dunn, and Daniel Noble. The experiments of Flourens and Hertwig have shewn that the hemispheres are insensible to incision or puncture, and that muscular contractions do not result from injury to the upper portion of the cerebral lobes.

As the grey matter of the nervous system is connected with sensation, so it is supposed to be the seat of the intellectual functions of the Brain; and in order to give this matter the greatest surface in a given area, it is placed on the surface of the Brain ; its numerous convolutions affording a still further extension of surface for the localization of the grey matter.

Consciousness and Will, like Intellect, are faculties allied to nervous matter, but of their nature we know nothing, and the phenomena are now only apprehended as ultimate facts.

The function of the hemispheres is to transform sensations into ideas, and to register impressions made on the senses. These impressions can be stored up in a latent state, and may be reproduced at indefinite intervals of time; a process which constitutes Memory. This power of recalling past impressions terminates only with life itself,

It is stated by Dr. Carpenter that, "the most philosophical method of tracing the connection between the nervous and mental functions is to investigate the relations between the *nerve force,* and the *mind force,* since either one of these can produce the other."

With respect to the link which immediately connects the materials of the Brain with the Mind, "it would be," as Sir Benjamin Brodie remarks, "as idle to speculate as on the proximate causes of Gravitation, or of Magnetic Attraction and Repulsion.

As every segment of the spinal cord, and every ganglion in common with the cerebrum may be considered as a centre of nervous force, and as every section of nervous matter, whether of the cerebral, sensitive, or motor system, is capable of performing the functions of the whole organ of which it is a portion, it is obvious that the ideas of Gall and Spurzheim of the necessity of independent localities for different manifestations of Mind, must be erroneous. It has, indeed, been abundantly proved by Dr. Roget that the evidence on which they and their followers have sought to establish their system is altogether equivocal and inconclusive ; and he has, moreover, shown that, even if we were to admit the correctness of their premises, their mode of reasoning from them is utterly fallacious, and justifies his remark that "with so convenient a logic, and with "such accommodating principles of philosophizing, it "would be easy to prove anything ;" and hence that their doctrine "should be rejected as having proved

* Physiology, translated by E. Millingan, M.D. p. 113.

nothing."* Magendie, also, a great authority on cerebral physiology, justly places the pretended science of Phrenology in the same category as the reveries of Astrology or Necromancy.

There are many Physiologists and Metaphysicians who deny the existence of reasoning power in the lower animals, and who consider that all their works are automatic or instinctive; but a little investigation will suffice to confute this opinion. There is no doubt that animals are endowed with Memory, and therefore, must possess ideas, and the power of associating those ideas. They form communities, they have social laws, and they have a language among themselves commensurate with their destiny.

The duplication of the cerebral hemispheres, each of which can act independently of the other, has given rise to Dr. Wigan's theory of the duality of the Mind; but their decussation leaves little room for doubt that in the normal state of the brain the hemispheres act in unison, and give force and precision to the mental operations.

In the volume of the cerebral hemispheres, histological anatomy teaches us that the nerve fibres amount to many millions; and we may presume that every fibre and cell has its appropriate action, and that the reasoning power is in proportion to the number of these organs.

In Metaphysics, various opinions have been entertained respecting the nature and number of our

* Encyclopædia Britannica, 7th edition, Article PHRENOLOGY.

C

fundamental ideas. These subjects have been investigated by Aristotle and Kant; the former has given lists of objects and their relations as bearing on our conceptions; the latter, of our conceptions themselves. The origin of our ideas has also been a disputed point. Descartes and Leibnitz, for instance, contended for the existence of innate ideas: Kant held a similar doctrine; Berkeley declared that matter exists only in our ideas: Locke traced all our ideas to sensation and reflection, and strenuously opposed the doctrine of innate ideas.

These examples afford a sufficient proof of the difficulties which embarrass the study of the Metaphysics of the human mind.

Every mental change is accompanied by corresponding chemical and electrical changes in the Brain; and this organ, like every other organ of the Body, is in a state of continual decay and renovation. This circumstance renders the power of reproducing former ideas, after an interval of many years, one of the most extraordinary, most wonderful, but indispensable provisions for the exercise of those powers of reason and of reflection by which Man is raised to the pinnacle of intellectual development, and acquires dominion over all the other forms of animal life.

Whether we direct our attention, with the aid of the microscope, to the investigation of the structure of the minute cells from which all organic forms are developed; or whether, with the telescope, we take a survey of the countless orbs in their progress through boundless space, and then contemplate the grand and sublime spectacle presented by the phenomena of the universe, where all is motion and change, and is governed by Laws unchangeable, we feel an irresistible impulse to exclaim

"O Lord! how manifold are Thy works!
In Wisdom hast Thou made them all!

THE END.

C. JAQUES, Printer, 30, Kenton Street, Brunswick Square.